SPIDER WEBS

BOOK 2 OF THE HILL LAKE SERIES

T.C. Lucas-Glass

ISBN: 979-8-9908545-2-9

Published in the United States by Lewis Lucas Glass Media, LLC

Dedications

This book is dedicated to my great-grandmother, Ora Lewis, whom I have only known through stories; my grandparents, Luratha Lewis, Walter Taylor Lewis, Sr., Lillie Bell Lucas, and William Hymon Lucas, Sr.; my parents, Earl and Marilee Lucas; my aunts and my uncles who all have contributed in seen and unseen ways to the shaping of my life.

Table of Contents

Chapter One

Starting Something

The sky was blue and the sun was shining. This Mississippi afternoon was just about perfect.

"They will be here soon!"

"I can't wait!"

"Do you think Erin will want her hair french-braided also?"

"It's going to be so much fun having a roommate!"

"Maybe we could do this every year?"

"Are they here yet?"

"Where are my walkie-talkies?"

Regina Lucas was bursting with excitement. She was 7 years old and an only child. She was gearing up for a very exciting summer. Her best friends were coming to stay for two months in Hill Lake, Mississippi. These were her 8 year old first cousins from Connecticut, twins Edwin and Erin Hunter. She envisioned a summer of swimming, riding bikes, fishing and catching lightning bugs. She couldn't wait to play princesses with Erin. Erin would sleep in the second twin bed in her room, and Edwin would sleep on the air mattress in the den where he could watch television late into the night. Their mother was Regina's paternal aunt, Belinda, who died during childbirth before Edwin, Erin or Regina could ever truly know her. That's actually not correct. They knew her through stories, pictures and the baby books she started for the twins while pregnant. The twins' dad was Edwin Hunter, Senior or Big Ed as everyone called him.

Belinda and Big Ed met in college at Tuskegee Institute. Tuskegee was somewhat of a Lucas family tradition. If you were born a Lucas, you went to Tuskegee which is why independent Belinda was determined to go to her mom's alma mater instead, Dillard University. After attending Tuskegee's summer science program for high school students, however, she was sold. The program allowed her to learn more about Tuskegee's legendary nursing program. She had always wanted to follow in her mother's footsteps and become a registered nurse. There she would excel and graduate at the top of her class. Big Ed took a more analytical path as a graduate of the accounting program. They married soon after college and moved to Belinda's hometown of Hill Lake to begin their life together. Big Ed decided to go into business for himself. He hung up his shingle for an accounting firm and Belinda worked at a gynecologist's office. They had lived in Hill Lake for two years when they found out Belinda was pregnant. The excitement was literally doubled when they discovered she was pregnant with twins.

"Twins are considered good luck around here," Belinda's mother, Mother Ora, used to say.

As a prominent midwife, she would know. The widowed Ora Lucas was the matriarch of the family. Her children and grandchildren referred to her as Mother Ora. Unfortunately, when the twins arrived three weeks early, Mother Ora wasn't in Hill Lake with Belinda. She was in Arlington, Virginia for the military burial of her beloved husband, Papa Will. He had died of heart failure two weeks' prior. So late in her last trimester, Belinda couldn't make the trip. Her brother, Robert and his new wife, Annabelle, were there to support Mother Ora. Big Ed stayed behind with Belinda.

"I should have been there," Mother Ora moaned at Belinda's funeral.

However, she conceded that everything seemed to have been done "by-the-book." She couldn't find any fault in the care Belinda received. After all, Hill Lake had one of the top hospitals in the south. In fact, a well-known HBCU medical school sent their residents to train there for years. Hearing it was "God's will" and that "Belinda and Papa Will were together" did little initially to soothe the searing pain Mother Ora felt in her heart. But over time, they were sentiments she held close to her. It brought her comfort.

After Belinda's death, Mother Ora pleaded with Big Ed to raise the twins in Hill Lake near her and Belinda's only brother. Big Ed was an only child. Understandably (and perhaps regrettably), Big Ed decided to raise the twins in Connecticut near his parents. He packed up and moved to Connecticut six weeks after they were born. Thankfully, the twins were healthy.

Big Ed and the twins had only returned to Hill Lake once. In the summer of 1977, they returned when Regina was born. The twins were barely toddlers and a welcome sight for all after so much loss the year prior. During that visit, Big Ed and Mother Ora argued when the topic of where they would live was revisited. Now, eight years later, the twins were finally returning for a visit.

The lack of them returning to Hill Lake didn't mean the Lucases and Hunters never saw each other. Quite the contrast, Regina and her parents, Annabelle and Robert, saw Edwin, Erin and Big Ed during summers and holidays over the years. They would travel to Connecticut or they would vacation elsewhere. Rarely, Mother Ora came along too. One of the most memorable vacations they had was to a newly-opened amusement park in Florida.

The pictures taken would give you the impression that it was the worst trip, however. Likely, that impression would come from a crying Erin being forced to take a picture with a lady dressed up as a giant mouse!

"I don't understand why he never comes here?" Mother Ora would often say to Robert. Was there lingering resentment that the kids lived a 3 hour flight away? Perhaps.

"Mom, he has complicated memories here. You must understand that," Robert reasoned.

Regina was hoping this visit would be the start of a new way to spend summers with her cousins. Since the twins had no memory of Hill Lake, she looked forward to introducing them to the hometown she adored. If they had a good time, she reasoned to herself, this would be the start of summers every year in Hill Lake.

There was another reason this summer was exciting; Regina was getting what she had hoped for the last couple of years. She was getting what she secretly asked Santa for last winter. She was getting what she would name after their dog, Spike — a sibling! Annabelle was in her last trimester and the baby was due any day now. This was the start of a new chapter for her family. It was the summer of 1984.

Chapter Two

Privately Dancing

Welcome

TO

Hill Lake

Largest US Black town; settled July 24, 1887 by former slaves of Masaw Plantation. Founded by the Hill Family consisting of Stancil & Lee Mary Hill.

Population: 4000

Hill Lake, Mississippi was a predominantly Black community formed by former slaves in 1887. The name came from a Native American hill (also called a mound) and a five mile lake in the town. The town had a public elementary school, a public high school, a catholic school, a hospital, many churches, stores and a community olympic-sized indoor swimming pool. Many residents worked at the schools, banks and stores in the town as well as on their family farms.

Papa Will Lucas ran the family farm for many decades. Inherited from his father, the Lucas Farm survived difficult environmental conditions including the harsh droughts in the 1950's when his kids were just children. Keeping with tradition, Papa Will attended Tuskegee Institute in Alabama.

Robert followed in his father's footsteps by going to Tuskegee along with his high school girlfriend, Annabelle. They spent the latter part of their high school years and early college years participating in many civil rights efforts, including voter registration.

Papa Will always said self-sufficiency was extremely important in society, so they focused on a future that furthered farm life. At Tuskegee, Robert studied Environmental, Natural Resources and Plant/Soil Sciences. Annabelle studied Agribusiness. They were a "match made in the middle of a soy field" as Mother Ora used to phrase it. When they graduated college, Papa Will retired and they took over the farm. Consequently, the Lucas Farm continued to be very productive. In addition to their livestock, they mainly harvested butter beans, soybeans and pecans. Seven miles south of Hill Lake, the community of Big Tree offered a state college, movie theater, countless restaurants and stores.

Growing up in Hill Lake in the 1930's, young Ora Lewis was considered highly intelligent and an exceptional athlete. Her mother, known as Lady Luratha, was part of the first generation born free in Hill Lake. Without a formal education herself, Lady Luratha made her children going to college a priority.   She was a business woman who ran the town's first hair salon out of an addition to her home. That way, she could keep an eye on her children and work while her husband worked in construction. Her savvy business sense helped their family afford to send all three of their children to college.

In high school, young Ora competed in state-wide swimming competitions. She was the captain of her high school swim team. She went into the military after high school as a way to save money for college. However, her military life was shrouded in mystery. No one is sure which branch she was in and Ora remains very tight-lipped about that time in her life.

After serving in the military, Ora attended Dillard University in New Orleans. While in college, she volunteered on the weekend with a search and rescue team on the gulf coast. After graduating from college, she disappeared for four years. That's correct–four years! Perhaps, disappear isn't the right word. No one knew where she was or what she was doing. Rumor is she was part of a secret elite underwater rescue unit during World War II. Would they have allowed women to do that? Would they have allowed a Black woman to do that? No one knew for sure.

Upon returning to Hill Lake, Ora spoke with an east coast accent. Perhaps, it was due to her senior year nursing training and graduate midwife training being in New York. She worked at Hill Lake Hospital delivering babies "from sunup to sun down" she liked to say. She hadn't been settled in Hill Lake long before she married Papa Will (may he rest in peace), and had Robert at the tender age of 40 followed a year later with Belinda. In her younger years, Ora loved to dance, especially the swing with Papa Will. Sometimes when she doesn't think anyone can see her, she silently, privately, dances the swing with an imaginary partner. This seems to happen inevitably when a certain blues song comes on the radio. She always kept a foot locker at the foot of their bed. "Memories of the past," is how she explained its presence. She still had it today, but no one dared to open it without her permission. She remained a woman of mystery.

During her midwifery years, Mother Ora, as she came to be known, delivered more than half the babies in Hill Lake over the better part of thirty years. She delivered three generations of children. There was even a time in the 1960's when a diva from a certain rhythm & blues trio from Detroit went into labor in Hill Lake. They were apparently on tour in the Mississippi Delta at the time. It was the talk of the town. Mother Ora delivered the baby girl and had a song named after her–something about babies and love.

She had many skills. She was an exceptional cook. She was known by family and friends alike for her homemade breakfast biscuits, pot roast and banana pudding. She used a lot of home remedies with things like tomatoes and potatoes. Mother Ora was a tall woman with a very straight posture who never let a thought in her mind go unexpressed. One thing she did not possess was a filter! But, everyone loved her for her unapologetic frankness which was never intentionally mean–just truthful.

When the twins and Big Ed arrived, Robert, Annabelle and Regina were there to greet them. As they walked to the farmhouse, the kids lagged behind. Erin noticed something in between two trees a few yards away.

"What is that?" she asked. "It looks like that leaf is floating in midair."

The kids ran toward the trees.

"It's just a spiderweb," explained Regina.

"A spiderweb!" screamed Edwin. He picked up a pebble and threw it through the web. "Take that, spider!" he playfully screamed. "I am the destroyer!"

"You are...something," said Regina. "Don't do that again."

"Why?" asked Erin.

Before Regina could answer, Annabelle beckoned them inside.

"We could have picked you up from the airport," Robert said.

"I know," said Big Ed, "but I want to drive through north west Mississippi on the way back. I hear some people are buying up land in that area for casinos".

"Casinos!" said Robert, "That would be impossible in Mississippi but, you never know".

Big Ed worked as a CPA at a big Connecticut accounting firm and always seemed to know things before they happened.

"You still have your ear to the ground," said an impressed Mother Ora as she walked into the room. She always liked to make an entrance. This time was no exception.

"What does that mean?" asked Edwin.

"Dad always hears stuff before everyone else," said Erin.

Speaking of hearing, Mother Ora could hear like a dog…or should I say an elephant…or maybe an owl? Her hearing was exceptional. Much to the chagrin of Robert and Belinda growing up, there wasn't much they could get past her. She could hear the muffled tears of Belinda when her first boyfriend ended their relationship, the strike of a match when Robert decided to try a cigarette and the last breath of Papa Will when he passed from heart disease. Her exceptional hearing was an asset for her and a roadblock at times for her kids. She didn't miss a thing.

"You two have grown so much, but you need some meat on your bones!!" exclaimed Mother Ora, "Aren't you feeding them, Big Ed? Come give me some sugar."

The confused twins embraced Mother Ora as she gave them both a kiss on their foreheads.

"Find your room and put down your bags," she said.

"Mother Ora, it is so good to see you," said Big Ed.

"It's overdue," said Mother Ora, embracing him in a big hug.

"I was nervous about coming," said Big Ed, "I just wasn't sure how we would be received."

"Why that's as silly as a hummingbird walking," said Mother Ora. Mother Ora liked to say unusual phrases. She really leaned into the southern expressions.

"I'm going to bed now. *You kids are always worrying me*," she said with a wink. That was it. That was the cue. The cue to tell you something or someone was making Mother Ora very, very happy. She was happy to have her daughter's family home. Everyone was under the same roof.

Chapter Three

Whispering Carelessly

Regina and Mother Ora were shelling butter beans on the farmhouse porch the next morning. Her parents, Annabelle and Robert, had gone grocery shopping and would be back soon. Having just finished breakfast, Edwin and Erin walked out on the porch.

"What are you doing?" Erin asked.

"We are shelling beans", answered Regina.

"Why?" Edwin inquired, "Can't we just buy them in a grocery store?"

"Of course you could, but that would make as much sense as hummingbirds walking", said Mother Ora, "You two sit down, grab a bag of beans and a bowl."

The twins soon found a rhythm in shelling.

"Can we eat these after we shell them?" asked Edwin.

"No. Absolutely not! They are butter beans. You may know them as lima beans. They are toxic if eaten raw. Do you know what that means? They are bad for you and could make you very sick," explained Mother Ora.

"Which ones are the toxic ones?" asked Erin

"To be safe, don't eat any of my beans raw!!" exclaimed Mother Ora.
She knew a lot about a lot.

After they had finished shelling their bags of beans for the better part of the day, Regina asked her parents and Big Ed if Edwin and Erin could go swimming in the town pool with her. The pool was open during the summer and only cost a nickel admission.

"Only if they have a lifeguard," said Big Ed, "The twins don't know how to swim yet".

"What?" said Mother Ora, rather alarmed. "That's outrageous. That's a shame!! Those kids are eight years old. What are you waiting for?"

"They have taken lessons several times at the Y, but they just haven't developed the confidence to try. It's okay though. I can't swim either and I have grown up to be a perfectly productive member of society," explained Big Ed with a hint of sarcasm.

"The Y? The Y! And you can't swim either? The Y does an excellent job of teaching swimming. Did you take them to all their classes? This makes no sense to me. I tossed Robert and Belinda in the pool when they were 3. Robert and I tossed Regina in the pool at age of 3. She immediately started dog paddling. She has been swimming ever since. After that, I taught her how to float, the breast stroke, backstroke and freestyle," said Mother Ora. As a former search and rescue diver and high school swim champion, she was flabbergasted that her own flesh and blood could not swim.

"No one does it that way anymore, Mother Ora. No one tosses kids in pools. That's just too dangerous," said Big Ed.

"Of course, we had someone in the water with them," said Mother Ora. "This is *Connecticut* parenting," she sighed.

Sensing a conflict about to arise, Annabelle decided to intervene.
"Hold it now; let's change the subject," said Annabelle. "After dinner, let's all relax and watch some television with the kids."

Later that day, as they sat around the television, a show the kids characterized as "for old people" began, complete with bubbles in the opening scene with orchestral music.

"Please can we watch Battle of the Television Stars?" the twins pleaded.

"What is that?" asked Mother Ora.

"A competition show with all three television networks," the kids explained.

So, the show began. The kids watched attentively as television stars from various popular shows competed in obstacle courses. As the night progressed, Mother Ora seemed to drift off to sleep on the couch. Drift off, that is, until the show's swimming competition began. When the referee blew the whistle *"tweet-tweet,"* she jumped up and mumbled something about being ready to dive. It startled everyone.

"3-2-1 we're off! 3-2-1 we're off!" she shouted.

Annabelle, Robert, and Big Ed gave each other a knowing look as Mother Ora continued to shout. Big Ed placed his arms on the shoulders of Edwin and Erin to reassure them. Shortly afterwards, Mother Ora sat back on the couch and was fast asleep and snoring.

"Let's get you into bed, Mother," said Annabelle, rousing Mother Ora to lead her to her bedroom.

"That was weird," said Erin.

"My mom said it happens sometimes with older people. They get a little confused at night after the sun goes down," explained Regina.

"That *was* weird. She sleeps a lot also," whispered Edwin.

"I think I'm ready to go back to Connecticut now," whispered Erin.

"Me too," whispered Edwin.

Mother Ora looked back at the kids. Of course, she heard everything.

Chapter Four

Unglamorous Living

The next day, the adults came up with a plan for the kids to spend time with Mother Ora on the farm. Annabelle, Robert and Big Ed had a long discussion with Mother Ora and Regina before the twins joined them for breakfast.

"I want my kids to understand where their mom grew up, " said Big Ed. "They have so many questions about her childhood on the farm that I can't answer. I'm hoping they can find the answers here," he continued.

"Mother Ora, this sounds like the solution is a farm tour," suggested Robert.

"I think that is an excellent idea," agreed Mother Ora.

"Regina and I will take you on a tour of the farm," the spry 77 year-old announced to the twins after breakfast. "It will be both entertaining and educational, so get out of those flip-flops and put on some walking shoes."

"Educational!" whined the twins in unison. "But, we're on vacation. Can't we go roller skating today?"

Roller skating was a popular pastime in 1984. Nevertheless, the farm tour commenced. As they walked the acreage, various crops grown on the farm were pointed out in great detail much to the twins' chagrin.

"These fields are our soybeans," explained Mother Ora. "We harvest them in early fall. They grow best in soil-rich, flat land like we have here in the Mississippi Delta. We count them as bushels."

"Dad said soy *milk* is going to become very popular one day," said Edwin.
"Your dad knows a great deal about many things," said Mother Ora.

Soon, their path took them in view of a beautiful body of water, the five-mile lake.

"I want to go fishing. Is there a boat where we can go fishing?" asked Edwin. "Dad got me a fishing pole for this trip and I can't wait to try it. He said there is a lake near here where he and mom fished often. He said he proposed to mom on that lake in a fishing boat."

"It sounded so cool when Dad described it," said Erin.

"That is the lake indeed. Fishing? Maybe later," said Mother Ora. "However, we have to wear life jackets if we go in the boat–even for us swimmers. You have to respect the water."

As they continued on their tour, they headed toward the pecan trees. The path took them past beautiful, large azalea bushes.

"These are my favorite bushes on the farm. These azalea bushes bloom for only one magical week every year. Usually it is around Easter,"

Mother Ora explained. "Their flowers are the

brightest pink."

Large spiderwebs could be seen between the azalea bushes. The webs glistened gold in the sunlight. Large spiders could be seen on the ground beside the bushes.

"What are those?" asked Erin.

"Those are the Keiko spiders. I believe they are from Japan. They showed up a year ago. Isn't that right, Mother Ora?" asked Regina.

"Yes, that's right," confirmed Mother Ora. "They make beautiful webs that shine during the day and sometimes glow at night. Look how they are shining!"

"Spiders!! Eeek!! Let's step on them!" screamed Erin.

"Yes, let's step on them," agreed Edwin, moving closer to the bushes.

"No! Stop!" Mother Ora shouted. "You never kill something just because you can. If everyone understood that, this world would be a better place. Are those spiders indoors? Are they blocking your path? Are they in any way destroying our property or hurting you? Then, you leave them alone! You have more respect for nature! Do you understand?"

"Yes, Mother Ora," the twins said with an annoyed tone. "So, should we just hate snakes outdoors?"

"Well, there are good snakes. Snakes that eat all the pests that could get in your house and eat the poisonous snakes that could cause you harm," Mother Ora explained. This response was met with silence.

The group headed back to the house. The twins lagged behind Mother Ora. Exasperated by what they felt was an unglamorous way of living, they plotted an escape from the bug-tolerating world that was the Lucas Farm.

"Regina, do you think we can go to the community pool tomorrow?" whispered Edwin while pulling Regina's arm toward them.

"Yes," Erin whispered, "I think we have had enough lessons from Mother Ora today."

"Guess what I'm going as for Halloween this year, Erin?" Edwin asked.

"What?"she whispered.

"An exterminator!" said Edwin in an exaggeratedly low voice. Erin giggled.

Regina looked at them. She was disappointed in what she was hearing from her cousins. Of course, Mother Ora heard everything.

Chapter Five

Not Going Crazy

The next morning, the kids went to the community pool. After paying their nickels, they went inside. Non-swimming Edwin and Erin were wearing floaties. Regina felt slightly embarrassed.

"Who are you friends?" asked Michelle, a neighborhood friend of Regina's.

"They look like babies!" laughed Ernest, the neighborhood trouble-maker.

"We're not babies!" said Edwin.

Despite not being babies, Regina, Edwin and Erin stayed on the shallow/kiddie end of the pool splashing and having an overall good time.

"Who wants to go fishing?" said Ernest as he made his way to their area of the pool.

"I do," said Edwin. "I've been wanting to fish since we got here."

"Me too," said Erin.

"A group of us are going tomorrow morning," said Todd. "You're welcome to join us. And tonight we are setting off firecrackers at the lake just after dark. If you aren't too much of a baby, come".

"We will be there," said Edwin.

As they were leaving the pool, they noticed a short man standing on the other side of the street loudly singing.

"Who is that?" asked Erin.

"I'm not sure," said Regina, "but I've seen him before".

The man appeared visibly drunk and dropped something in front of Edwin as they both crossed the intersection.

"Sir, you dropped something," said Edwin.

"It's not mine," the man said.

Edwin picked up the item. He was taught not to litter. It was a shiny whistle sealed in plastic. He had seen the type as a prize in his cereal box. It was the type a school coach would use.

"Tweet-tweet," the drunk fellow sang, and stumbled past him.

Not seeing a trash can nearby, Edwin shoved the whistle in his swim trunks pocket.

"Come on. We don't want to be late for dinner".

Back at the house, the adults inquired how their day at the pool was.

"We got invited to go fishing on the lake," said Erin.

"Absolutely not," said Mother Ora. "Until you learn about water safety you should not go anywhere near a lake. I'll start teaching you tomorrow".

Shortly after, she was fast asleep snoring on the couch.

"Mother Ora is right," said Robert. "No fishing in the morning."

The twins protested but were quieted by their father.

"I'm afraid I agree with your grandmother and uncle. I believe I have been too lax in making sure you knew how to swim and all aspects of water safety. We are going to change that. Come tomorrow, I'm going to have you take beginner swim lessons at the pool here under the supervision of Mother Ora. I might even take lessons myself," Big Ed conceded.

"A beginner's class. That's embarrassing. Everyone will think we are babies!" protested the twins.

"Then you will be babies that can swim," retorted Big Ed. "We are going downstairs to the basement to listen to that new song on the Memphis radio station. Do you three want to join us or stay up here and watch television?"

"Watch television," they said in unison. "Let's see what's on tonight."

Annabelle draped a blanket on Mother Ora as she slept on the couch, then joined Robert and Big Ed. The three adults headed down to the basement chatting about the new song's singer as they descended the stairs.

"Can you believe she used to sing at lounges around here?" asked Robert. "Her career has been quite impressive."

"I'm just glad she got away from *him*," said Annabelle. "She is so resilient. I guess love really had nothing to do with it." They all laughed.

"What are they talking about?" asked Erin.

"The new song by that lady with the big hair," said Regina.

As soon as he thought the parents were out of earshot, Edwin whispered, "I think we should go to the lake to watch the fireworks".

"Are you nuts?" said Regina. "Did you not hear the adults? And neither of you can swim."

"We will wear lifejackets," said Edwin. "Come on. They said we couldn't go fishing. No one said we couldn't watch firecrackers," he reasoned.

"That is because they didn't know about the fireworks," said Regina.

"Please," pleaded Edwin. "I don't want to go alone, but I will if I have to."

Reluctantly, Regina and Erin followed Edwin out the door. They loaded the lifejackets on their bikes and rode the path down to the lake. Once they arrived, they got in the boat and pushed away from shore.

"Let's put on our life jackets," insisted Regina.

"Okay," said the twins.

When Erin picked up her vest a large Keiko spider was on it. She shrieked, stood up and dropped the vest in the boat. Edwin grabbed the oar and stood up also, violently swinging the oar in an attempt to kill the spider. In the process of his swinging he accidentally hit Regina in the head knocking her out cold. She collapsed in the boat, the boat rocked and Edwin and Erin fell overboard.

"Help!" screamed Erin. "I can't see anything! It's too dark!" Storm clouds had covered the once shiny moon.

Suddenly she saw a light, a green light, a green log, a glowing log. She flapped her arms in the water as hard as she could in the direction of the glowing log. She soon discovered it was covered in fluorescent spider webs. She grabbed it and saw spiders scurrying into the water. She gripped it tightly as the boat drifted away with unconscious Regina. She searched the water and saw Edwin kicking feverishly to stay afloat.

"Edwin, grab my hand!"

Edwin reached out and Erin pulled him closer. He held onto the log as well. No one could hear them as they both tried to shout amidst distant thunder. Edwin remembered the whistle in his pocket. He pulled it out of his pocket and bit off the plastic covering. Then, he blew and blew and blew.

"Let's try to use the log to make it to shore," said Edwin. He was so disappointed when Erin showed him that the log was part of a larger branch underwater. It wasn't going anywhere and to make matters worse– it was getting slippery.

"No one knows we're out here," Erin cried. Edwin blew and blew and blew.

"3-2-1 we're off! 3-2-1 we're off! 3-2-1 we're off!" Mother Ora shouted as she sat upright on the couch. Of course, she heard everything.

Chapter Six

Thrilling

"3-2-1 we're off! 3-2-1 we're off! 3-2-1 we're off!"

So loud was Mother Ora that the three adults came running to check on her.

"We have to go," she said.

"Mother Ora please calm down," implored Annabelle as she looked around the den, "But, wait, where are the kids?"

"I'm calm," said mother Ora, "We don't have much time to get to them".

After a quick assessment and seeing the bikes were gone, they realized the kids had left.

"Annabelle, stay here in case they come back", said Robert.

Mother Ora, Big Ed and Robert took off on the path looking for the kids.

As they rapidly walked the paths on their acreage, they began to notice the Keiko spiderwebs were only glowing on the right side of the path.

"That's the way to the kids!" exclaimed Mother Ora, "follow the light!".

The fluorescence of the spider webs led them through the woods to the part of the lake where the kids had entered.

"Is this even possible?" asked Big Ed.

As they got closer to the lake, it began to rain. Among the thunder, they heard whistles and screams. They picked up the pace.

As the whistle sounded through the cold, wet night, Edwin exhaled and said, " I don't think I can blow anymore."

"My arms are tired," said Erin.

Suddenly they heard shouting.

"3-2-1 we're off! 3-2-1 we're off! 3-2-1 we're off!"

"Regina!"

"Erin!"

"Edwin!"

Then suddenly they heard a splash. And another. Mother Ora and Robert were swimming in the water. As Mother Ora swam past a clump of cattails, Edwin, who was closest to her, came into view. She quickly pulled him by the arm and tucked her arm under his. Robert (who swam considerably slower than his mom) met her on their way back to shore.

"Where is Regina? And Where is Erin?" he yelled.

"Take him ashore, I'll go back for the girls," Mother Ora directed.

She swam back toward the cattails but there was no sign of Erin. The glow of the fluorescent spiderwebs on a few of the cattails illuminated a shivering Erin holding on to the back half of the log which was splintering. Saying nothing, she grabbed Erin, tucked her under her arm and swam ashore.

"Mother Ora, Edwin just told me he thinks Regina is in the boat. I'm going to..."

Before Robert could finish his thought, Mother Ora was back in the water, swimming to the boat to get Regina. Regina was arousing as Mother Ora literally flopped herself inside.

"What is happening?" asked a confused Regina.

"Hush, child. Mother's here. You are going to be just fine. Everyone's okay." With those soothing words, Mother Ora embraced Regina, assessed the bump on her forehead then rowed them back to shore with the remaining oar.

Grabbing beach towels from the trunk, everyone quickly loaded in the car to get home. But, as they arrived home, another surprise awaited.

"I called the ambulance; they are on their way, but I don't know if they will make it in time. My water broke as soon as you left to look for the kids. I didn't want to leave until I knew the kids were okay. My contractions are now a minute apart,"rambled Annabelle bent over in pain.

"Let's have you lay down, sweetheart. Let Mother Ora take a look," Mother Ora said reassuringly. "Robert, put some ice on Regina's forehead. Big Ed, get blankets for the kids."

As the ladies went to the bedroom, the dads got to work. Big Ed got blankets for the wet kids, and Robert made an ice pack for Regina. Although the room was quiet and no one said a word, it was evident all thoughts were remembering Belinda.

Naturally, Bid Ed was having flashbacks. The kids were recalling the stories.

"Mother Ora has delivered more babies than the stork!" Robert said to lighten the mood. "I'm going to check on mom," he told Regina with a reassuring hand on her shoulder. As he headed to the bedroom to check on Annabelle, he heard the siren from the ambulance approaching outside. Opening the door, two tall paramedics greeted him.

"Please come in. My wife is in labor, and my daughter had a bump to the head," Robert said panicked.

As soon paramedics entered, a most-welcome sound came from the bedroom. The sound of a baby crying. Mother Ora came to the bedroom door and announced, "it's a boy!" Robert rushed into the bedroom.

"Mother and son are just fine," Mother Ora assured everyone.

"We'll take it from here Ma'am," said one of the paramedics. The paramedics joined Robert, Annabelle and the baby in the bedroom. Soon afterwards, one of them came out to assess Regina.

"Seems like she may have a mild concussion," he concluded after examining her. "I've cleaned the scrape on her forehead. Let's keep doing the ice packs and keep her up for a while to watch her. Call us if you need us."

Thanking the paramedics as they left, Big Ed sent the kids to go get their showers.

"And wash your hair!" shouted Mother Ora as she collapsed on the den chair. "What am I thinking?" she suddenly asked herself as she quickly stood. "I shouldn't be sitting on this furniture in my wet clothes! I need to take a shower as well. Robert, help me to my room. I have told Annabelle she needs to keep plastic on this furniture." Robert laughed as he helped his exhausted mother-in-law to her bedroom.

The next morning, the house was filled with chatter as Robert and Annabelle entered the kitchen with the new addition to the family.

"We are naming him after a very important member of this family. Meet baby Reginald Oratio!" they said in unison. Mother Ora smiled. After everyone had a chance to see the baby once again, questions from Regina, Edwin and Erin resumed.

"Grandmother, tell them about your swim meet," requested Regina.

"Were you really a spy during the war?" asked Edwin.

"Can you teach me how to crochet?" inquired Erin.

"Did you *really* deliver that diva's baby?" Erin asked curiously.

"Mother Ora, please tell us," the kids pleaded.

Mother Ora smiled and said, "I will answer all of your questions if you teach me how to do that new dance called the lettuce- patch or whatever the name of that dance is," she said.

"I'm so glad we're here," Erin whispered to Edwin.

"Me too," said Edwin.

"You know, maybe moving down here would be good for the twins," Big Ed whispered to Robert.

Of course, Mother Ora heard everything.

"You kids are always worrying me," she said with a wink.

THE END

Afterword

This work of fiction was inspired by my great-grandmother Ora, a midwife; my grandmother Luratha, a businesswoman ahead of her time; my grandmother Lillie Bell, an educated teacher, and my mother, Marilee Lucas, RN, a proud graduate of Tuskegee Institute.

Additional inspiration came from my children, my siblings, my hometown, and the spiders that populated our backyard during the summer of 2024.

Our seniors are a valuable source of knowledge and history.

Talk with them. Learn from them. Cherish them.

Thank you, to all the translation resources out there.

T.C. Lucas-Glass

About Our Author

T.C. Lucas-Glass is an author and physician originally from Mound Bayou, Mississippi now living in Atlanta, Georgia. This is her second book in *The Hill Lake Series* with her first book being the popular short story, <u>Butter Pecan: Book 1 of The Hill Lake Series.</u>

The Adventures in this Special Town Continue…

Book 3 of The Hill Lake Series coming in 2026!

Visit
www.lewislucasglassmedia.com
for updates!

www.ingramcontent.com/pod-product-compliance
Lightning Source LLC
Chambersburg PA
CBHW051926220626
47052CB00003B/599